Is Happiness Worth The Pain?

Michael A. Young

Royal Media and Publishing
P. O. Box 4321
Jeffersonville, IN 47131
502-802-5385
http://royamediaandpublishing.com
royalmediapublishing@gmail.com

Cover Design: Bill Lacy Designs

ISBN-13:978-0-9987154-0-7
ISBN-10:0-9987154-0-9

Printed in the United States of America

Table of Contents

Prologue

It was a calm, warm night in the city and in a well-known, but in a not so good part of town. A car was park by the curb with the motor running. Nothing about this scene seems strange, especially at 1:00am on Thursday.

Also this wasn't a very populated neighborhood. This street in particular had a lot of abandoned homes, and the ones that were lived in weren't looking too much better than the empty ones.

Scattered about here and there in some of the yards were old useless vehicles. By the look of them the neighborhood kids had found uses for them by turning them in to club houses. What ever happened to tree houses? Guess you actually need trees for tree houses.

In the darkness a boom-boom was heard in the distance. A car appeared slowly. Couldn't really tell what kind of car it was. That was because of all the aftermarket crap on it, oversized tires and rims, big grill and all factory symbols removed or painted over.

The car slows even more and pulls up next to the one parked by the curb. The window comes down and a cloud of smoke flows from inside. Won't say what the smoke came from, but it wasn't a cigarette or regular cigar. In the midst of the cloud a face appeared. A young man perhaps 18 or 19.

With a cough he asks the unseen driver of the parked car "yo, partner, ya'll know where Dory street be at round here?"

Receiving no answer the teen spoke a little louder and said "Hey man! Where Dory Street at man?"

Still no answer from the parked car. With a shout of "Fuck you then!" And "Retarded ass nigga." The face vanishes within the cloud of smoke. The window raises and the car is gone with screeching of the tires.

Silence returns to the mostly empty street. The lone car now begins to show movement. As the driver door eases open a pair of beautiful brown legs swing out. A woman extends her full figure out of the car and looks around for any other unwanted attention. Standing at 5'9" she turns to check herself using the reflection in the driver window. Looking at the burgundy silk blouse she had on she adjusted herself to make sure not too much was showing. She had heard on many occasions that she was blessed with breast. Wanting to make sure the girls were up and perky and not just hanging out. Smoothing out the wrinkles in her black pencil skirt, she gave her thighs a pat. Running her fingers through her shoulder length black red streaked hair, she turns to look at the numbers on the houses. Moving forward, the 6" heels she wore echoed through the night.

Pinpointing her destination she approached a house that didn't seem to look as bad as some of the other surrounding homes. Yet, it still wasn't a place she wanted to be seen going into during the day time.

Taking a very deep breath she attempted to summon up the courage to ring the doorbell. With her finger lightly touching the button, a voice in her head said "Don't degrade yourself like this. You are so much better than this!" With chills and almost fright, she jerks back her hand and spins away from the door. In a retreat she runs to her parked car. Well, she runs the best she could in those heels.

Inside the car now, she starts the engine and stomps on the gas. Tearing down the darkened street as if she was been chased, 20 minutes or so later she parks in front of her own townhouse. Still not the best in the city, but nice. Much nicer than the housing area she just left. The Vargus apartments were kind of small, but quaint. Relieved by the sight of the well-lit and full parking lot, she got out and made her way to her home. This had been her home for the past year or so.

This woman is in her mid-30's and had just moved away from a roommate that was a friend of a friend. She has a small group of friends that has been together since high school and also went to college together. Four of them in fact. After college, they all chose life directions but remained close and tight as they were in high school.

Taking out the keys to open the door, her cell phone rings. Looking at the caller id, it's the person whom she just left waiting.

Entering the house, she waits for the ringing to subside. As it finally does, she calls her best friend in the world. It's just about 2am now, but she knows she'll answer. Because she knew what was supposed to go down.

"Bitch!! You either better be in trouble or just had blown your back out having sex."

“Neither. I got cold feet and bounced."

"Shanette! I knew you would chicken out! A late night one-time sweat feast ain't your style. What he say when you left him hard and dry?"

"Didn't even make it in Dominece!"

"Damn....You did bounce!"

"What am I going to say to him at work tomorrow? I go right pass him first thing when I get there?"

Just then her phone beeped. Taking a seat on the end of the bed, she looked at the incoming call’s number. Putting the phone back up to her ear, she says "Girl it's him, Victor.”

"Can you put him on 3 way?" Dominece asked

"Sure. Why?"

"You got me up now. Let's have some fun."

"Hold on." Says Shanette to Dom as she clicked over. "Hello?"

The other voice says, "What's the problem girl? You didn't get intimidated by all this did you?"

"Hold on please." Clicking back to her friend, "Girl! He's trying to mack with some tired Barry White voice."

"Click me in!" Dominece said in an excited voice ready to play.

"Hello. I'm back. Sorry 'bout that. What were you saying?" Shanette asked in the sexiest voice she could use without laughing.

"I know I'm packing, but I didn't mean for you to have day dreams and get scared. I could take it as slow as you want." The guy said.

"Oh really?" She answered. "Something came up, so I stayed home."

"What's wrong? Couldn't find anything big enough to stretch you out far enough to get you ready for this tree limb?"

"Hell to the Nah!" Came another voice over the phone.

With surprise in his voice, the man lost all the baritone growl in his voice. And asked "Who that? Who's that other voice?"

"I'm what else came up. I got what she needs more than you player." Dominece said with sarcastic tone.

"What you mean? What you talking 'bout? Netti Nett wha she mean?"

"I told you I don't like it when you call me that. My name is SHANETTE!" She said with a slight hint of anger.

"I give her all she needs, and more. I came by, and you got canceled. Plain and simple."

"SHANETTE! You get down like that!!" He asked with amazement.

"Well....."

Cutting her off, Dominece says, "Yes! We both switch hitters. And right now, you are interrupting us!"

"Whoa. For real? Can I come and join in?"

"I don't know. What you working with?" Dominece asks. "We are both used to 10' or better."

A pause passes, then the man responds "You two are in luck. I got 13inches ya'll can share." In that deep voice again.

Shanette drops the phone on the bed and begins to kick and roll around wildly trying to contain her laughter while holding her mouth.

Dominece on the other hand didn't even try to hold her amusement. She laughed right into the phone. "I tell you what. We're already into it, but we'll leave the phone on and you can listen."

"That's cool, but first things first. I know what Shanette is working with. She thick. But what you looking like?"

"Baby. I'm dark chocolate, big ass titties and an ass you could serve drinks on."

"You cute?"

"Nigga, I'm a star. I could be a model, but I don't want to do all the traveling. "

"Oh shit!"

"Come on Dom. I'm tired of waiting." Shanette says playing along.

"She's good and wet already. How ‘bout you daddy? You ready?" Dominece asks talking like a phone sex girl.

"HELL YEAH!" He answers.

"Ok. Let him hear it baby," Dominece whispers.

Click!

Together in unison, the women explode in laughter. Both being grown women doesn't mean that from time to time they couldn't have a little adolescent fun at some jerk's expense. Well, long as it was harmless to everyone involved.

"Dom, you are a mess. I could never have thought up that stuff on my own." Shanette said, as she wiped away tears.

"We had him going, didn't we? Bet he was at home ready to rub a big one out." Replied Dominece still giggling. "Well we better get off the phone and go to bed. Still got to work in the morning.....You know what?"

"What Dom?"

"Guess who I heard was back in town for business? Sure someone would love to see his Shay Shay." Dominece cooed.

"Well I don't want to see him! Now I gotta get this few hours of sleep, so I won't choke a bitch today."

"Heard that. Good nite girl."

"Nite."

After showering and getting in bed Shanette laid curled up in bed clutching her pillow. From the time she hung up with her friend, she thought of him. His face, his body, the fun times they had and also the very real pain of betrayal. Finally she drifted off to sleep on a tear soaked pillow, but this time the tears were from sorrow not joy. In her sleep one word was repeated several times....ANTHONY.

Chapter I

Fresh Starts

Downtown was buzzing with people scrambling from here and there like bees in a hive. In the day time, there were always commuters around. But around noon lunch time especially on Fridays, it seemed the whole city got hungry and had to eat in various places in the heart of the city. In the summer, restaurants adjusted for this lunch time hunger blitz by adding patio seating. Even the fast food joints accommodated patrons with picnic style umbrella tables. It was mostly business men and women who frequented the fast food spots. Always on the go. Always in a hurry. In their lingo, they're called movers and shakers. Never having time to sit and enjoy the food. Just order, eat and keep it moving. Most would only visit the upscale restaurants if they were trying to woo a client or seal a deal.

In the midst of all this chaos downtown, Shanette was looking up at the addresses on the sides of huge glass and steel towers. She has lived here all her life, but never really had a need to enter any of these buildings. She felt like somewhat of a tourist wandering aimlessly back and forth across streets. With the assistance of a friendly security guard on break, she was pointed in the direction of a black glass building that stood out from the much larger and average buildings surrounding it.

Passing through the revolving door, the first thing she noticed was the cool air. Her old job in a factory, where her best friend Dominece still worked had zero cool air. Unless you count the dry air that was blown throughout by ceiling mounted fans, the place was much bigger on the inside than it looked from the outside. Walking over to the building directory, she searched for where she needed to go. She had an interview with a small modeling agency there in town. The agency would do print work and commercials for state wide companies, locally owned businesses and magazines. Also small franchised stores who needed faces and bodies to promote their sales. Plus using local unknown models, these companies saved a ton of money. Besides, all these Tyra Banks and Tyson Beckford wannabee's believed this kind of work could spring board them to major work in much bigger cities. All Shanette wanted was a different direction in life.

As she walked and searched for the elevators, she noticed the looks on the people’s faces that were around her. None looked very happy. Could they be as unsatisfied with their jobs as she was in the factory? She felt many things day in and day out at the factory, but fulfillment wasn't one of them. Deciding to use the degree she had in communication, Shanette took a pay-and-walk package they were offering to try and reduce personnel. It was enough for her to get her own place and buy a car. The rest was in the bank, just in case getting a new job took longer than planned. Luckily, it only took a few months between leaving the factory and this interview.

The phone interview went great she thought. Now the question is, can she be just as impressive in person as she was on the phone?

Then from somewhere close, she heard "Excuse me! I'm right here! You don't have to look any further!"

The voice snapped Shanette out of her thoughts. Also wondering from who and where that obvious fake low toned voice came from. Looking around she met eyes with the security guard over against the wall behind a small desk.

"That's right. Here I am, come claim your prize." The security guard said, as he stretched his arms in her direction.

Taken back by this bold and lame attempt to get her attention, she decided to show him some. And not the attention he wanted. "Are you serious, you jerk ass motherfu...."

Cutting her off he says, "Hold on Hold on. Before you get mad I was just clowning around. Didn't mean no harm. You just didn't seem to be as uptight as the rest of these gargoyles in here".

"Sir, I was about to let you have it! You lucky I have an appointment to get to".

"My bad. I apologize ma'am. My name is Victor, but everyone calls me V. How can I help you? That is, if you actually need help that is."

"That is much better. My name is Shanette. Shanette Tolls, and I have an interview on what looks like the 3rd floor at the Donovan Agency.
"Oh a Model!"

"No! Interviewing for an Assistants Job."

"Could have fooled me. Standing there looking like a mocha skinned 'Beyoncé." The elevators are over there around pass those giant fake potted plants."

"Thank you for the help. Oh, by the way. Turn down the clowning a little. Hate for you to joke with the wrong chick in bitch mode."

While waiting on the elevator to open she heard, "Good luck Netti Nett." Turning, she says in a firm voice "That ain't my name Victor!"

She enters the Donovan Agency after being buzzed in by the receptionist. Shanette noticed the office had a different vibe to it. Different than the cold marble, glass down stairs. Here soft music played and not that elevator music some offices play. She heard a jazz instrumental of R Kelly playing. Nice. From somewhere she could smell scented candles. Like the scent of honey and cinnamon rolls. "Wow. That's an odd combination, but it works in here." Plus it made her hungry.

"Yes? May I help you?" The secretary asked.

"Yes. My name is Tolls, and I'm here for...."

Just then a man spins out of an open office door adjacent to the front desk. He was a tall white man. Looked like he fell right off the pages of GQ. Very handsome and wore a suit that looked tailor made. He stepped toward Shanette and began to circle her.

"Mr. Arms. This is Ms. Tolls. She's here for..."

Raising a hand cutting off the secretary in mid-sentence. He finally stopped circling and said, "Nice facial features. Complexion isn't perfect, but fair. Hair color can be worked with. Very top heavy and healthy backside, but that seems to be the norm in this city."

The man wasn't from here. She could tell by the obvious accent. Maybe up north. New York maybe. At least nowhere near the south here.

"We may have work for you in our plus size division. Leave your head shots and number here with Toni, and we'll get back with you if we can use you." He said with an air of arrogance.

"Mr. Arms! Ms. Tolls isn't here for a modeling job. She applied for the assistant job. Besides, she is not PLUS SIZED, I AM."

Shanette looked at the secretary. She was on the heavy side, but presented herself very well. Not at all a sloppy big woman.

Continuing her rant, she says "Around here we call her size thick! Something a man can hold on to. Nothing like those toothpicks you're used to working with in New York."

"Miss Tolls, I want to apologize to you for my criticism. That's my job here."

"That's ok. Really. Happy to be thought of as a model."

"And to you Toni.." he sticks his tongue out and vanishes back into his office closing the door.

Eyes wide, Shanette turned back to the secretary and said "Did he just stick his tongue out at you?"

"Don't mind him, he's harmless. We are serious about our business, but we also have fun around here too!" Toni said with a smile. As Toni led Shanette down the hall, she noticed that Toni wasn't wearing any shoes. She was walking barefoot on the soft gray carpet. The back office had no door and the entrance was much bigger than a regular doorway. Behind a massive mahogany desk sat a shapely woman. Graying hair, but a fresh from the stylists look. Skin color was about the same as Toni's, if not a shade darker. She stood as Toni introduced Shanette.

Pleasantries were exchanged. "This is Mrs. Donovan, CEO and owner of The Donovan Agency".

"Ms. Tolls. I have looked over your resume and application. Very impressive. I see you quit your job at the factory. May I ask why? I believe they pay very well!"

"Yes they do, but we earned every nickel we made. Working with your hands, standing on concrete or metal floors for 10 hrs. a day 6 days a week isn't for everyone. I could do it, but I felt I was wasting unused abilities Mrs. Donovan. I just got tired of being a human robot." Shanette answered.

"I see." Said Mrs. Donovan leaning forward. "A very understandable answer. Much better than someone saying they're bored. You believe there is more to you and for you. Excellent. You are not the first to apply from the factory, but you seem to be the best qualified. I would love for you to find the job fulfillment you're looking for here with us. Also I would love to tell you that you could start Monday morning, but I can't." She pauses and looks into Shanette's eyes.

Sadly Shanette replies "I would like to thank you for taking time to consider me for the position and it was a pleasure meeting you. And you as well Toni." With a genuine smile she adds, "Have a wonderful day."

As Shanette turns to head to the front waiting area she hears “You have an outstanding personality, even at the thought and hint of rejection."

Pausing, she turns and says "Thank you. One must remain professional at all times."

"You learn that at the factory or in a college course?" Mrs. Donovan asked with a smile.

"That's just the way I am." Shanette says, also with a smile.

"Great! Can't wait to get started working with you!" Mrs. Donovan proclaims as she stands and extends her hand.

"I..I don't understand. You said..."

"Yes. I said, I couldn't let you start Monday. But be sure to be here at 9am Tuesday. See, Monday is my birthday and that’s a holiday around here! This year I will be 62."

Running over to Mrs. Donovan, she shakes her hand then Shanette tells them “Thank you so much, and you won't be sorry about the decision. Smiling as they watched her leave, Mrs. Donovan says to Toni "I got a good feeling about this Ms. Tolls."

"So do I Vikki, so do I." Toni said as she left the back office and walked to her desk. At that same moment, the closed door across from the desk reopened and Mr. Arms stepped out. "Toni, has my appointment shown up yet?"

"No. Not yet."

"Lazy unprofessional southern women!" He said while straightening his tie.

With quick steps, Toni rushed the man swinging her arms and shaking her head. The attack looked serious, but each blow actually landed with baby like force. With howls of laughter, Mr. Arms covered his chest pretending to protect himself.

Coming out the back office, Mrs. Donovan watched the commotion. "Jack! What the hell is going on up here?"

But Toni answered before Jack. "He said southern women are lazy!" And went back to the wild swinging.

Mrs. Donovan runs forward saying " Oh hell no!" Flinging her arms around like Toni.

Fending off the comical assault, Jack made his way back into his office and closed the door again. "Damn women." He yelled through the door. "We love you Jack." The two women said in unison and making kissing sounds. He answered through laughter "I know ladies I know, and Jack loves you too. I just feel sorry for Ms. Tolls. Knowing you two, she'll be beating me up too." Voice trailing off he says, "We need more men around here. I need back up."

Shanette exited the elevator with a visible spring in her step. Ignoring all the stone faced on lookers that passed by she felt like she was floating on air. This was the start of her dreams coming true. A career, not just a job. A career with a future. Her smile got wider as she sang under her breath Jill Scotts. Hate on me Haters,' but her groove was broken by the security guard Victor. "That's right ma'am shake that tail for me." Looking over in his direction she noticed the fool put a dollar bill in his mouth. He almost caused her to get an attitude.....almost. Now swing her hips and ass purposely she switched over to him. Bent down to his ear and said "Vic. That's right ain't it? Hear this. I wouldn't use that dollar to wipe my ass let alone shake my ass for it." Raising back up and turning towards the front door she heard Victor say, "That's right. Talk dirty to Vic." And he slapped the desk and laughed. She giggled to herself. Not because the comment was funny, but because the man really didn't know how much of an ass he was really being.

In the car Shanette makes a call on her cell. A few rings and the voice answers "What trick?"

"Call the crew it's time to party." Shanette says.

"The fuck 'em gear or the stop the show gear?" Dominece asks.

“Cameras flashing, dudes shuddering gear." Shanette coos.

"You got the job bitch?!"

“Hell yes!!"

"BITCH!!"

"I know, we gonna show out all weekend."

"It's on then. I'll call the crew. Flashing lights flashing lights." Dominece said excitedly.

Shanette hung up and started singing Kanye Wests ‘Flashing Lights’

Chapter II

The Crew

The music was so loud you couldn't concentrate on your own thoughts. Multicolored lights blinked on and off all around and bodies looked like they were moving in slow motion. Almost naked women bounced, shook and gyrated. Men mostly looked robotic with their basic two step. Here and there, you could spot a couple of feminine men dancing like women.

In the middle of all this excitement was 'The Crew.' A four woman crew composed of Shanette, Dominece and their two other girlfriends Anita Watts and Robin Lock. These four women were close as sisters. Also they argued like sisters too. Shanette and Dominece had been friends since jump ropes and jacks. They met Anita and Robin in middle school, and became 'The Crew' officially in high school. Matching jackets and outfit colors during any school event or games. Everything young women did in the late 80's and early 90's.

Robin Lock was the only one in the group to have settled down and got married to a man that stole her heart in junior year of college. After graduation they married, but didn't let that put a hold on their dreams. Basic and ordinary, but dreams all the same. Robin always wanted to be a nurse and followed through with it. Her husband, Gerald Lock had always been good with cars such as body work and engine repair. So it was no surprise to anyone that he became a master mechanic. Able to get top dollar at any place that did repair work. He decided to open his own shop and be his own boss. But was sometimes called by local dealerships to work on the most difficult repairs. They had a good life together and were trying to have their first child.

Anita Watts was the most dramatic, flamboyant, self-absorbed woman any of them had ever known. Any other group of women wouldn't be able to deal with her for more than an hour, but these women knew Anita's heart. They knew deep down she would give you her last drop of blood if needed. Only to a select few mind you, but she had that compassion in her. Anita loved attention. It could be good or bad as long as she got it. She would do almost anything to get a man’s eyes on her especially. A sexy stroll past him. A brush of her ass against his hand. Or sometimes she would resort to the dropping of something in front of a guy, bending over and pretending to struggle picking it up in order to get him to pick it up for her. Now, not all the guys she flirted with made it past the flirting stage. Some were just play things used to past the time. Anita's main goal was to get a man with money. To say she is a gold digger was mild. The rest of ‘The Crew’ joked saying she kept a pick axe and shovel in the trunk of her car. Always looking for an upgrade in men. In her own words she would say "a good man can do a lot for you, but there is always a better man out there who can do more".

'The Crew' sat at a table in the middle of the club right where they knew they would have the most visibility around the club. All four were dressed to be noticed. Shanette wore a dark blue skirt, black and blue top with blue 3 inch heels. Dominece had on a jet black pants outfit with a gray lace top covered by a mid-length jacket. Robin, the conservative one in the group was wearing a stone gray dress with spaghetti straps. Always concerned she was bigger than she really was, covered her upper body with a long white silk shawl. Now Anita being the scene stealer, she is had on a fire engine red see through top. No bra, but enough designs to hide her areolas. The outfit could get her arrested for indecent exposure if it was worn in the day time. But you know how dimly lit clubs are.

With music pumping, drinks flowing and spirits high, this night was made for celebrating. Shanette's new job, Robin being promoted to head nurse and Dominece celebrating because she didn't have to whoop a bitch at work this month. Anita was celebrating that once again she updated her man status going from $90k to $100k a year. A $10k a year difference may not seem like much to some people, but to Anita, that much more meant at least $6k a year that could be spent on her that the old guy couldn't spend.

After a couple rounds of drinks, and flirting by all girls, even Robin. But that was with her husband when he came after work playing stranger in the club. The Crew decided to call it a night, because the DJ announced last call and their weekend fun money was running low. Leaving out they walked as a group with Gerald in back. Even without him they moved together. No one walked alone. This night, Gerald being the gentleman he was, stayed till all women got in the cars and drove past him and blew. Shanette and Anita waved, robin blow a kiss and Dominece flipped him the finger. But it was all in fun. She was like the little sister he never wanted. As Shanette headed home, she thought what a wonderful way to kick off the start of a new beginning.

20 minutes later, phones began ringing. All checking in with Shanette, because she lived the furthest away. One after the other, "You home?" "You make it in?" "Bitch, you better be home by now!" Getting in bed she thought, they are crazy and wild, but I love my girls.

Chapter III

New Beginnings

Tuesday morning and downtown is alive with motion. Cars scurrying around like giant bees. People with their coffees or energy drinks get themselves hyped up for the long work day. Serious faces on all men and women in business suits. Their facial expressions only change because of phone conversations. In the midst of all this was a pretty face with a bright smile. A lone woman spoke to everyone she made eye contact with. Very unusual actions for this section of town unless it was business oriented. Wearing a powder blue suit jacket and a knee length white skirt with light blue pinstripes, she headed for the building that held the start of a new life for her. Once again, the security guard Victor sits behind his desk and admires the women in the lobby. Mixing in with a crowd of men that were quite tall, she moves past Victor without him noticing. He was trying to look up the way too small skirt of a woman who just dropped her briefcase close by. This helped Shanette in her evasion efforts.

Upstairs in the Donovan Agency, Vikki gave Shanette a formal tour of the office. There was a break area complete with full size refrigerator, a couple of microwaves, 4 tables with 3 chairs at each and a 42 inch TV mounted up in the corner. A very nice restroom in the middle hall way. Another 2 offices besides Vikki's and Jack Arms offices sat in the back across from the CEO's office. Both were very nice. Either could be a head boardroom in any tower around town. Vikki told her to choose. Either one or both would be suitable for her job title. 'Chief Executive in charge of business relations.' In other words she is in charge of convincing clients to work with the agency. This was something that needed to be done that no one else really had time to do. Mrs. Donovan handled the money portion of the business. Mr. Arms groomed and prepared the models for their shoots, and made sure they were there before time just in case any unknown problems arise.

The secretary Toni Jerson was in charge of interviewing potential models; hiring a select few and clearing out the wannabes and ain't never gonnabees. So an executive of business relations was desperately needed, and Shanette felt blessed to be filling it. In the office she chose, sat alone leather chair with a book on it. The book was that of office furniture. With a confused look on her face, she turn to call for Mrs. Donovan. Just before she could, Vikki appeared in the doorway. Around here we decorate our own labs.

"Labs?" Shanette asked very puzzled.

"Yes labs. Laboratories are where you put in serious work. Not just work. And clients will judge your appearance first. Since you will be representing a modeling agency you must look immaculate. Then your lab, office will be judged. Then your negotiating skills will seal the deal or have you in my dog house." Mrs. Donovan says.

"I understand now. Don't worry I won't disappoint you Mrs. Donovan". Shanette replies.

"I know you won't. Otherwise we wouldn't be having this conversation. By the way when you get the chance take a peek at Jack's lab. Very masculine and very impressing to young women". Vikki answers.

"So I should decorate feminine, but pleasing to a man's eye," Shanette says giving a sly smirk.

Bumping Shanette with her hip, she puts her hands behind her back and leaves the office saying "Very good Ms. Tolls. You catch on very quick. You are going to fit in just fine around here honey".

Sitting in the chair and opening the catalog, Shanette grins and spins around like a kid. When she faces the doorway again she jumps startled. There in the doorway stood Jack Arms red with laughter and holding his mouth.
"Mr. Arms...I am so sorry. That was very unprofessional...."

"But highly entertaining. Ms. Tolls, we are not that stuck up in here. Inside these walls it's very leisurely in here. Unless you are with a client, then strictly business. But since no one is here yet..." just then, Jack throws an empty water bottle at Shanette and runs off like a school boy shouting "Welcome Ms. Tolls".

Eyes wide and mouth gapped open. She sat there stunned. After taking the playful act in, she rises up and snatches up the bottle and runs toward Jacks office. "Mr. Arms, I'm going to fill this bottle with cold water and get you back".

Time passes very quickly and Shanette excels at her job. She impresses client after client with her charm and business knowledge. Some even brought other business associates to the meetings. Now these associates had no plans on using The Donovan Agency or using models for the matter at all, but Shanette was so engaging they would schedule a meeting of their own to discuss what she could do for them. Mrs. Donovan was extremely pleased with her work. Unable to move up title wise, she received bonus after bonus. She brought in so much business more models had to be hired. Toni and Jack were pleased because more business meant extra time working. Play time slowed due to the busy days, but sneaky tricks still got played. Mrs. Donovan kept saying, all work and no play meant low pay and high tempers. Believe it or not, she was the biggest joker of them all. Doing things and blaming others, then sitting back enjoying her handy work.

One afternoon right before quitting time, Mrs. Donovan stood in Shanette's doorway smiling. "Ms. Tolls, I have a client for you".

Is Happiness Worth the Pain?

"Ok? What is it about THIS client that is making you smile like that?" Shanette asks curiously.

"This client isn't the wealthiest or representing a major company, but he could be bring a very high profile business opportunity to us and the city. Word on the business circuit is we are the hot business to call if you're looking to be noticed, and you are the person. Woman! Who can make it all happen."

"Great. Should I expect to be working over today? "

"No, no. He wants to meet with you for lunch tomorrow if possible. Is it possible?"

"I can move my current appointment to an earlier time."

"Excellent. He wants to meet at DeAgos by the waterfront at noon". Mrs. Donavon explains then leaves out the doorway.

"Vikki?"

"Yes Shanette?"

"What is his name? I may need to know that. Plus, I need to Google him to get to know him in advance."

"I'm sorry. Too excited I guess. His name is Mr. Regal. Anthony Regal".

Chapter IV

A Regal Appointment

The DeAgos, is an Italian restaurant that sat on the waterfront surrounded by a well maintained open field park on both sides. It had a high class golf course look. Some would come and just get carryout and eat at tables in the park. The restaurant was huge, but kept a healthy crowd. Reservations weren't necessary, but did help if you didn't have a lot of time. Food was excellent. A variety of dishes and spice variations with genuine Italian wines.

Shanette sat waiting at 15 minutes till 12:00 eating cheese and sipping a lemon water. She was never late because that made a bad business look if the client had to wait on the representative. Sitting in a booth she watched the door wondering what Mr. Regal looked like. She had different approaches for each client. A client in an expensive business power suit, meant she would not be very aggressive. She would let them believe they are actually laying out the specifics of the contracts. A regular suit meant open negotiations. This person would be more likely to be flexible in hammering out an agreement. Anything else. A t-shirt, or heaven forbid tracksuit meant this client more than likely wasn’t serious about making a deal. So time for them is cut down.

Not many men came in that had that ‘let’s make a business deal’ look. Until this guy walked in wearing a steel gray suit with a navy blue shirt and a blue and white striped tie. He had a very confident look and walk. He greeted the hostess with a bright smile. Then she pointed him towards Shanette's booth. He approached Shanette and greeted her with that same smile.

"Hello. My name is Anthony Regal. Would you be Ms. Tolls from the Donovan Agency?"

"Yes I am. Pleased to meet you." She says as she stands to shake his hand.

"Please, be seated Ms. Tolls the pleasure is mine. I hope I didn't keep you waiting long?" He says as he slides into the booth across from her.

Shanette notices he's not wearing a power suit, but a very, very nice everyday work suit. If the numbers can match and the representation of the model or models is right, this meeting should go very well. She pulled out a tablet that she had next to her on the seat as he ordered a salad and soft drink. She asks "Mr. Regal? Do you have a written proposal for the need of our models? I don't see a brief case."

"Yes I do. Like you, I see less is more. The need for a brief case is very outdated." Anthony says as he pulls a slim tablet from his suit coat.

Impressive Shanette thought. Especially the way that suit fit him and still had room for that against his body. Not that she was checking his body out, but his form was definitely noticeable. Athletic and well-toned. Works out often and believes in keeping himself well groomed. But this isn't a date, this is business. And even in her wildest fantasy, she couldn't date him if he asked. Her own personal rule...don't date a client or coworker. With rapid blinking, she snaps herself back to the business at hand. "Yes that's right. Technology demands that you stay current or stay in the stone age." Then she pops open a stand for the tablet and sits it down then smirks.

"I totally agree Ms. Tolls." Regal says, as he puts his tablet in front of him. Then he pulls out a small box and plugs it into the tablet. With a swipe and click. The tablet image appears on the flat wall surface in the booth.

"Is that a?" Looking closer. "A projector?" The smirk disappears and excitement replaces it.

"Yes it is." Smiling and slightly blushing. "As you said. You can't stay in the stone age."

As they talked and Regal ate, they discussed his need for models. He was opening a nightclub. Business casual, from 6pm to 1am. Nothing like anything that has been in the city before. The models were needed to bring people in. You never see commercials for nightclubs, but for his club, you will. It was genius. Great way to get people in. Better than word of mouth.

As the waitress comes to refill his glass, she knocks his glass over and it spills in his lap. Shanette and the waitress jump.

"Oh my God, I am so sorry. Please let me clean that for you" the waitress says.

Shanette didn't do it, but felt just as embarrassed as the girl. Oh no. This may be a deal disaster, but before she could apologize Anthony says “Don’t worry about it. The water is clean and so is the suit. I've had water spill in my lap before and I'm sure it will happen again. May I please have the check?"

"Yes sir." The waitress says with her head down.

"Ms. Tolls, can we finish this in your office? Perhaps later today?"

"Yes of course. I'll be there for the rest of the day, and please allow me to pick up the check. I insist. "

"Ok, as long as I get the tip. That poor waitress was traumatized." Mr. Regan says as he stands.

As she returns with the check, Shanette lays down her card and Mr. Regal slides a $100 bill in her hand. "Don't be so sad. Accidents happen. No harm done."

"Thank you sir, thank you so much."

"Until later Ms. Tolls." Then he turns to leave.

Noticing he left his projector she calls him and says, “You left your.....”

"Keep it. Technology demands we stay current." He smiles and leaves the restaurant.

Thinking. This is no ordinary client nor ordinary man. Just then the waitress returns with her card. "Thank you. Please come again, and I want to apologize again. He just...hmmmmm. He was just too fine."

"Yes he was. Maybe too fine."

Chapter V

What You Going to Do?

It's the weekend and as usual the Crew met up for an after week, before week drink. This time they're meeting at Robin and Gerald's house. The Locks live right outside of what is considered downtown. This part of town is what you can say is the common part of the city. Most people there had decent enough jobs. It made for a more neighbor than hood. Lawns are maintained by the home owners and or the kids in the neighborhood. At least one car in every driveway and garages scattered here and there. Small front yards, but nice sized backyards. The Locks were fortunate enough to have a backyard that had a view of a park. So on many summer evenings the Crew would gather here to admire or clown the people coming and going through the park. Because Robin loved her backyard so much, her husband Gerald had a deck built and bought furniture for it.

Shanette sat in chair next to a deck bar that Gerald had just added. He thought of himself as an unlicensed bartender. Truth of the matter is he didn't really know how to make that many drinks. The ones he did make up were real strong, so no one called him out on his self-entitlement. Robin sat next to Shanette, while Dominece stood at the fence yelling at the men who were jogging or riding bicycles. Not having a backyard since she lived at home with her parents, Dominece never sat still. Always moving around. She only sat still when her buzz got too intense for her to function normally. When that happened, look out. Anyone in blurred eye sight and listening range was blasted with all kinds of foolishness. Jokes, insults, hugs or hard ass slaps. But it all was done in fun and Dom always apologized in her own way saying, "Ya'll bitches know, I'm just shitting with ya'll."

Gerald being the true gentleman he is, would gradually make his drinks less lethal as the night went on till he was just serving out water or straight soda. The girls loved him like the big brother he acted like. And he felt like the big brother. Especially when the whole Crew went out. But at home he could rest a little easier. Robin never worried about any of the girls trying to get with him. Not that he was unattractive. He was very handsome. Standing at 6'5" and weighting a good 255 lbs. Dark skinned and muscular. He kept his form from his years playing college football, but got hurt his sophomore year and began to concentrate on a career other than sports. Even back then he played guardian to the girls. There were plenty of jerks and forceful boyfriends to deal with. Now...Anita was different. She didn't worry about Gerald, but she did keep her eye on her. Anita was a money hawk. She went after the guy with the most money. Now Gerald wasn't in her financial range, but he was far from your average 9 to 5 guy.

Is Happiness Worth the Pain?

Coming back to the bar, Dominece called to Gerald. "Brother G. A sister needs a refill on her Henny and Sprite."

"Coming right up Dom." He answered.

"Dom? How many of those have you had?" Shanette asked.

"Just opened my 3rd 5th for her drunk ass." Gerald said sticking his head from behind the bar.

"Whatever shit bird." Dom answers, throwing an ice cube at him from her empty glass.

"For your info MOTHER!!! This is my second Henny. Those 4 beers earlier don't count," saying as she plops down on Shanette's lap.

"Get your big ass off me girl. You know this chair can barely hold all this ass of mine, so yours added is guaranteed a trip to the ground."

Looking at her watch, Robin says "Speaking of asses. Where the hell is that trick Anita at? We have been out here 3 hours already and she was supposed to bring the steaks for grilling."

"Calm down baby. I got burgers and links on the grill now."

Dominece says "No Robin is right. That bitch volunteered steaks and I want mine. She probably somewhere with meat in her mouth now, and not the kind we're waiting on. Well maybe later, but a bitch is hungry for a rib eye now."

"Whoa need to know info, and I didn't need to know some of that Dom." Gerald said as he headed over to the grill.

"My bad G." Dom says as she began to laugh.

Just then Anita comes through the side gate door with a man in tow. She was wearing a very small skirt. It only came to the bottom of the curve of her butt. If she bent over all her goodies would be there for the world to see. Her top wasn't any better. Light green, sheer, sleeveless and no bra. Anita wasn't as amply built as the other girls. More centerfold model than everyday thick as most women are. By it being warm and the start of summer, the sheer top was acceptable. With her lack of tits, no bra could have passed. But not in front of Robin's husband. The brown skirt was only proper for bedroom play or the strip club. The man on the other hand looked very nice. Knee length white shorts with a light gray button down silk shirt. White and gray low cut shoes.

"Bitch! What the fuck you got on? Or don't have on better yet. Nobody here wants to see or smell your nasty wet ass!" Dominece shouted from her seat across from Shanette and Robin.

Not embarrassed in the least. Anita spun around showing all her outfit. "Yes. I just threw on a little something today. It's so warm out, and I hate for sweat to run down my legs in shorts. Besides, Frankhere said he loves to see my legs."

Robin moved around in her seat obviously uncomfortable and slightly embarrassed. Being a very conservative woman wearing a knee length pair of beige shorts and brown tank top. She took a quick sip of her drink and said to Anita "So glad you could make it. And with a guest too. Would have been nice to have known you weren't alone, but welcome....ahh..?"

"Frank, Frank Brimm. I am so sorry about this. I thought I was expected since Anita told me to be sure not to forget the steaks."

"She had you buy and bring the steaks? You are a piece of work. This trick bitch was supposed to bring the steaks. Over an hour and 2 drinks ago." Dominece yelled before shaking her glass at Gerald again smiling.

"Don't matter who bought them whore, they are here now. Big G, could I have a damp panties?" Anita replies.

Frank hands the steaks over to Gerald and shakes his hand apologizing again with an embarrassed look on his face. Following him inside, he leans forward and asks "What is a damp panty?"

Laughing, he answers "It's a drink I threw together one day. Gin, a shot of 151 rum and a half shot of pure grain mixed with a cherry Pepsi. I limit the ladies to no more than 3 of them. 2 if they have already been drinking."

"Does it work? I mean does it get a woman wet?" Frank asks bearing a huge grin.

"Slow down chief, it works. In Anita's case, she will spill a drink in her lap or." Leaning closer, he whispers "or she'll piss on herself again and say she spilled her drink," winking and elbowing Frank in the arm.

Now as the guys talk among themselves in the house the women begin to talk about the week's gossip. The happenings in the factory, who's in the hospital and why, Franks net worth and his soon to be replacement, and this very interesting man that has Shanette puzzled. They discussed the meeting at DeAgos and the meeting that had to occur later that day at the Agency. How he looked, where he was from, how many kids, was he married, how much money did he have and did it look like he had a big dick was all questions that were asked. Shanette answered what she could as they sipped on their drinks.

A car horn blared from the park and a faint voice called out, "Yo! Yo! What's going on?"

Dominece swirled the ice in her cup and called out "Big G. A sister is in need of a liquor fix. You want a bitch to dehydration out here?"

Coming out the back door with fresh bottles of liquor and a bag of ice, he is followed by Frank with the steaks seasoned and placed on a tray ready to be grilled. Refreshing everyone's drinks, Gerald heads to the grill with Frank and cracks open a beer. During their time in the house, Gerald finds out that Frank has had his car serviced at his shop before, but it was his younger brother who dropped it off. No repairman in the state could get his car running the way it did when it was brand new except for Gerald. Being guys, their talk outside was cars and sports. Telling Robin about the new information about Frank kind of eased much of the tension that was there earlier.

"And as I walked him out, he asked me out sort of." Shanette says.

Almost choking on her drink Dominece jerks forward and says, "Bitch! You better have said yes!"

"Hefa, he invited me. Well me and my girls to the opening of his night club Chocolate Silk. We get the diamond V.I.P treatment. Private room not a roped off section, but an all glass room with its own bar and waiters. He said, “It's for entertainers that come in town." Shanette says snapping and waving her hand,

"How many get to come?" Robin asks looking a little worried as she looked over at her husband.

"As many as I want, but it will be The Crew, Big Brother G, any man Dom may want to pull out her ass and who ever you're with at the time Anita. I'm not taking advantage of Anthony's generosity. So if it's not Frank, keep it here on the table." Shanette says looking at all the girls and starring at Dom.

"I won't say shit, but what if he does ask you out for real? What you gonna do?"

"I guess I'll find out if it happens" she answered then finished off her drink.

Finally after some time, the men bring the meat over to the patio table. Raising up they hear the horn and faint voice from the park again. Annoyed Anita lets out a deep sigh. Looking at her, then Frank then back to Anita. "Has he met Pit yet?"

"No! And hope to God he never does. Why Dom?" Anita voices with attitude and a frown.

With a grin and a look over her shoulder in the sounds direction "Who do you think is doing that shit!?"

In unison the rest of the group except for Frank grumble the word, "Fuck!"

Is Happiness Worth the Pain?

Frank leans over to Anita and asks “Who the hell is Pit?"

Chapter VI

The Silent Office

It's Friday morning, and Shanette is on her way to work thinking of the question Dominece hit her with last weekend. What if he did ask her out? What would she do? Would she answer right away or take some time to think it over? Is it even permitted to date a client? Yes, Mr. Regal is very handsome and sophisticated. Very different from the kind of man that she usually attracts. Like that clown Victor in the lobby. Underneath the pickup lines, he may actually be a decent guy or he may just be a real honest ass. Now Mr. Regal, Anthony seemed genuine, but he could be hiding a secret or two. Or even a secret family. On the other hand, he could be an honest to goodness white knight in shining armor. After a few more minutes of questioning and answering herself she completely didn't notice she walked past Victor. Up the elevator and was swiping her card at the Agency door.

The obvious absence of Toni Voss's and Jake Arms bickering snapped her out of her internal questioning. No models waiting. No music playing. Where is everyone? Looking at her watch she saw she was actually 10 minutes earlier than normal. Then she heard soft voices coming from Vikki Donovan's office. In the hallway, she could now here three voices. Two women and a man.

"Vikki have you been back to see the Doctor?" Toni asks gently.

"Yes Toni, and nothing has changed. No worse." Vikki answers through heavy chest coughs.

"But not any better either love. Last month, you were coughing up speckles of blood. Now, you're coughing up globs of blood. Blood honey, that's not good no matter how much the amount." Jake says looking at Vikki like a worried dad.

"Yeah that's true. But don't count this old bird out yet. I still got some flight left in these wings. Ya'll keeping this to yourselves. I don't want Shanette to worry also. Bad enough you two know as much as you do. She is young and doesn't need to have me to worry about while she is finding her way." Vikki said drying tears from her eyes and looking at all the blood in her handkerchief.

Being quiet as a field mouse Shanette stood against the wall wrapping herself with her own arms. Holding back tears, she gathers herself and approaches the office door, loudly. This was to alert everyone to her coming presences, so they would think the conversation was still private.

"Hello? Is everybody back here?"

"Yes doll. We are all back here." Jack answers. Being the only one able to speak right away without a cracked voice.

"Everything alright? What's going on?" Shanette asks trying to sound convincing in being unaware.

"Oh, everything is fine. I got choked, and our EMS team came running unnecessarily to my aid. But I guess it's better to be safe than sorry."

Looking at Vikki through red teary eyes Toni adds " yes it is better to be safe than sorry. You keep that in mind next time you....ah have an attack like that again. Excuse me sweetie." As she moves past Shanette, "It's almost time for business hours."

Jack still looking worried and not trying to hide it says "I'm not going out for lunch today. So if you need your EMS team, I'll be here all day. "

Reaching out and squeezing his hand for reassurance and gratitude, she says "Thanks Jack! For everything!"

After Mr. Adams leaves, Shanette sits down and forces a smile past wanting to cry. "Yes honey. What can I do for you?" Vikki asks back in her usual pleasant tone.

"I have a question. A question on our policy. Rather just random curiosity. Is it ok or evenrinsespermitted to date or meet with a client on personal time?" Shanette asks nervously.

With a huge smile, Mrs. Donovan leans forward and says “If he asks or has already asked, go for it. If I was a tad younger, I would be after him myself."

"Are you sure Mrs. Donovan? This wouldn't be bad for business?"

"Only if you let it on your end. That's why it's called personal time. Do what you want and with whom ever. After the work day ends, your time begins." Vikki answers.

"He hasn't, yet. But it's good to know I have that option."

As Shanette stands and leaves Donovan's office, Vikki rises and opens a bottled water. Before she could take a sip, she coughs and uses her hand to cover her mouth. More blood. Thick blood. Looking up she whispers “Jesus! Jesus! Help me Lord." Then turns on the office music, locks her door and sits down on the floor in a corner and cries.

Chapter VII

Meeting Pit

It's opening night for Chocolate Silk and it seems like the cream of the city has come out to experience the club. There are a few night clubs scattered around town, but nothing like this. It was built on a vacant lot. Nothing around but parking spaces. So no drunk or disgruntled patrons could cause any damage to anything. The entrance had a red carpet on a black painted side walk. It was also covered with a full length lighted awning. Very clever. Even if it's raining you could still stand in line to get in. No doorman, just a digital counter over the door. When capacity was 10 people under full it would stay closed till people exited. The nearest fire department had a remote to open this door from the outside in case of an emergency.

Inside the lights were low, but not dark. On each side of the club was a long bar. In the center was the dance floor. Only it was lower than the regular floor by 3 feet. Steps down circled the dance floor all the way around. Plenty of room to walk around. Tables were placed in the rear between the bars and chest high cocktail tables were everywhere. But please. No liquids or food on the dance floor. Waiters and waitresses wore blue pants and white shirts with blue vests, so they would be easy to spot. Of course there was security. They wore black pants with their choice of shirts with ties that read security.

No dress code to speak of, but casual to business wear was suggested. Most complied, but the ones that didn't felt so out of place they would leave to change clothes. Entry price was only $10. So paying to re-enter wasn't a big deal because this place was worth it. The DJ had a booth over top the entrance door on the 2nd floor. Up here was the DJ and the V.I.P areas. 2 on each side up there and in the rear upstairs was the V.V.I.P area. A glass enclosed booth with a private bar and server. Only Mr. Regal and the club manager had access to this room.

This is where the Crew is enjoying the night thanks to Mr. Regal's personal invitation. The ladies are definitely dressed to impress. Shanette is wearing an emerald green strapless dress that plunged midway down her chest. The dress hugged her hips and flared slightly at the calf. Dominece had on a black top that covered one shoulder and left the other bare. It was see through right at the cleavage, but didn't expos anything vital. To finish off the outfit was a black and white bold stripped skirt. Robin being surprisingly out of the norm. She wore a peach suit jacket with peach pants. Gerald being the complying husband, had on a basic black vest and pants with a peach shirt. Now Anita...! She bulged eyes with an off the shoulder crimson red top that crisscrossed her breast with sheer silk around her midsection. For the bottom, she also wore a skirt. But it had splits that should be on the sides. She turned it to have the splits going up the front and back. No stockings and more than likely, no panties.

They drank, danced, sang and enjoyed the hospitality. Mr. Regal was a most gracious host, making sure everything and every need was taken care of. As the women went down to the dance floor, Gerald accompanied Mr. Regal, Anthony as he told him to call him to the bar. As the guys drank and talked, Frank came in. Gerald waived him over and introduced the two. Anita didn't invite Frank, but he heard about the grand opening and stopped in to get a look around and a drink. Never taking his eye off the Crew, Gerald had a sudden cold chill go up his back. Squinting to look through the crowd he spotted a familiar person. Wearing basic khakis and a white button down, the guy didn't really stand out. He just seemed odd.

A little louder than he wanted, Gerald said "Oh shit! It's fucking Pit!"

Anthony asked, who was Pit? Frank also added the name Pit because it came up at the cookout. Gerald explained, Pit was an ex suitor of Anita. His bank account shrunk though due to bad stock choices and Anita's interest went along with the money. Problem is, he didn't take the rejection well. He never got physically with her, just very annoying. To whom ever she was with though, was another matter. He once threw a bowling ball at a guy while leaving a black tie banquet. The guy dropped Anita the next day.

"Holy shit!" Frank said downing the drink he was sipping.

"Should I call security over?" Anthony asked.

"No, no. I got it. It's 'bout time to call it a night anyway." Gerald said.

Frank asked, "Is his name really Pit?"

Laughing, Gerald said "No. The girls call him Pit, 'cause he acts like a pit bull. Once he locks on, he's hell to get away from and he kind of looks like one too." Frank slapped hands with Gerald, shock Anthony's hand, exchanged business cards and left. The two men went down to the ladies shielding them from Pit's view. They explained the situation to the girls, then headed up to get their things. As they exited the club, Anthony took Shanette by the hand.

"Ms. Tolls. I hope I'm not being to forward, but I would love for you to accompany me to dinner at DeAgos. This time as a date rather than a client." Anthony asks with slight grin on his face.

Without hesitation, she replies "Yes. Anthony, I would love that." Releasing his hand, she rejoins her friends. Looking back, she smiled at him and gave a wink.

Chapter VIII

Where Did He Come From?

Shanette wondered around her place, as she talked on the phone to Dominece and Robin. By this being her first date with Anthony, she was very nervous. She brushed her teeth 3 times and changed clothes too many times to count. Sending selfies to each girl to help her decide on an outfit. A nice simple purple and white blouse and basic black jeans was chosen. It wasn't too revealing, but it did accentuate her breast and ass very tastefully. Dominece actually suggested she wear a top that dipped right above the belly button exposing more of her cleavage. Only, well not only. But the major problem with that was, her chest was too big for that. It would have just managed to cover up her nipples. So that was a no go. Robin's suggestion was a full business suit.

Just as she finished getting dressed, her phone beeped. It was Anthony asking if she was ready. He told her to come outside the car was waiting. Clicking over to the girls, she told them later and she would call when she got back. Grabbing her keys, she wondered why he didn't say I'm waiting outside. Opening the door, Shanette damn near dropped her purse and keys. Sitting there waiting on her was a Jaguar limousine. Anthony stepped out, after the driver tipped his hat and opened his door.

"Surprise! I hope this isn't too much. I like to make a good first impression on dates. Just a second! Before we leave, I have flowers for you."

Blushing, Shanette says "That is so nice of you. And no this isn't too much. Just have never been on a date like this before. Matter of fact, I have never been in a limo before."

Coming up to her, he handed her a bouquet of roses. But these roses were made out of crystal. Eyes wide, Shanette was speechless.

With a broad smile he said “These are just as beautiful, but will last a lot longer. Hopefully you will think of me every time you glance at them!"

"Anthony! You are unbelievable. So far you have blown my mind with this limo and crystal roses."

They entered the limo and was off to dinner. At DeAgos, they were seated right away. Pulling up in a limo helped. As they sat and ate, they communicated with each other quite easy. Shanette told him about how she was hired at the Donovan agency, and about the people that worked there. He talked about the other clubs he opened in other cities. They even discussed passed relationships. Normally a big no no on a first date, but each felt so at ease with the other, the topic wasn't that big of a deal. Shanette told about the jerks that cheated on her. A few even tried to get with her girlfriends on numerous occasions. Anita may have fucked one, but she couldn't prove it. And they both denied they found the other sexually attractive. Anthony admitted one of his exes managed one of his clubs out of town. She had finally moved on, or so she told him. Bottom line she was a damn good manager. And he always had an assistant deal with her to make things easier.

This info made Shanette a bit hesitant. How often does he go check on that club and is he telling the truth. Shaking her head to mentally clear her thoughts, she told herself we are not together. It's just a dinner date. It never has to go past this night. But looking at him while he ate, she thought if it did go past tonight how would she handle that?

"Is everything alright? Shanette? Shanette?"

"Oh I'm sorry. Yes I'm fine. Mind just wandering is all." She answered.

Leaning back, he says "Oh My, Am I that boring?

"No no. My mind was on you. Sorry to say my attention at the time wasn't. You are far from boring. In fact I am really enjoying your company. "

"Well Shanette, that is most reassuring. Honestly I was a little nervous about tonight. It's been a very long time since I meet a woman that was almost perfect. Goals in life your reaching, beauty, intelligence, and importantly single."

Wiping her mouth and raising an eyebrow, she said "Almost? What is it that you think I'm missing, Mr. Regal?" That last part was said with a slight attitude.

Grinning, he answers. "You're not a billionaire. You're not able to sweep me off my feet and take me away from my mundane life. You're not, are you?"

With a giggle. "No. Not yet. Sorry, but you'll be working Monday morning. "

Lightly banging on the table he says, "Well shit! Ms. Tolls, I believe I will continue trying to woo you. I see great potential in you, and I would love to see such a lovely flower bloom into her future."

"You are very charming Anthony. Bet you are used to having girls eat out of your hands? May even have one in every city you manage a club."

"No on both counts. I don't really like to mix business with romance."

"You mean pleasure!"

"No romance. You can pleasure yourself very easily. That act has nothing to do with romance. Romance is an issue of the heart."

"Wow. Never heard it put that way before, but you are absolutely right." Shanette says holding up her glass in a toasting fashion.

They continued to eat and talk. The conversation she overheard at the office also came up. He suggested she tell her boss she overheard and was extremely concerned. She said she would do just that first thing Monday morning.

As the night ended the limo stopped in front of Shanette's place. Being a gentleman, Anthony led her up to her door arm in arm. She turned around and looked into his eyes. Holding his hands, Anthony stepped closer. Putting his hands around her back, Shanette tilted her head back and closed her eyes. He took the opportunity, and....blew on her cheek making a farting sound. Immediately she laughed. He laughed also.

He moved back and grabbed her hand. Kissing it, he says "The night has been so great, let’s end it on a less taxing note and we’ll save that act for another evening."

"That sounds perfect Anthony. Next date. Good night Anthony."

"Sweet dreams Shanette." Before he entered the car he said, "Hopefully the dreams will include me somewhere in them."

Waving, she says under her breath “Bet your ass I will." Then she turned and went inside the building.

Chapter IX

Pleasure or Romance

Shanette thought for a hot second. Opening the door to call Anthony back, she jumped back. He was there in the doorway. Before she could inhale his soft lips were on hers. Not wanting to resist she gave him her mouth. Tongues flicked and darted between their mouths. Shanette placed her hands around his back feeling the tight muscles in it. He placed his hands on her hips then up her sides. Picking her up with incredible strength and gentleness, Shanette felt herself get a little wet.

Wrapping her legs around his waist, Anthony began to carry her to the bedroom. Removing his lips from hers they stop in the hallway. Looking into her eyes he says, "I need it now!" And set her down.

"What do you need now?" She asks. As soon as she had finished the question, he put his paws down the back of her pants and pulled them down exposing a black lace thong. No longer wondering his need, she laid back against the wall.

Anthony takes a half step back to look at her magnificent body. "I don't know if I should touch you or kiss you from your feet to head."

Giving a very seductive look, Shanette says "Do whatever you want!" Looking straight at the growing bulge in his pants. She then rubs his chest and ripped up his shirt. He didn't have a movie perfect body, but damn if it didn't beat any regular man's frame. No 6 pack, but ironing board flat. No love handles and a nice chest. Shanette moved to kiss it, but he eased her back against the wall.

Bending down to her chest level, he placed a hand under each thick thigh and lifted her in the air. Placing a leg over each shoulder he began to kiss the wetness of her panties. Supporting her weight with the wall he broke the thin string going up her ass. Breathing heavy, she was in a state of half shock and half ecstasy. It took a few seconds for her to realize she was sitting on his shoulders.

Putting his nose under the destroyed panties, he kissed her low lips. His tongue felt like warm silk against her peach. At first, he licked and massage her pussy with his mouth. Then he slide his tongue deep inside her. This made her explode. A slow and steady stream of sexual juice flowed into his mouth. Cupping his tongue Anthony scooped her cum up and swallowed it all. This continued for 15 more minutes or 3 orgasms. Shanette's mind was so blown she couldn't tell the difference.

After eating his fill, he lowered her back down. "How was that?" He asked whipping juice off his chin.

"Unbelievable! Let me see what poked me when you let me down." Bending down on her knees, she unzipped his pants. Without a need to reach inside, his thick penis was already through his boxers. It wasn't super long, but it was very thick. Even half hard. "Wow. This is more than a mouthful." Placing a hand at the base of the penis, she opened up and took the thick sex muscle in her hot mouth. Like a cold Popsicle on a warm summer night, she sucked and licked. Slow then faster. With each downward motion, he grew bigger and harder. Moaning, he ran his fingers threw her hair.

"Damn that feels so good. I can't take much more before you make it cum." Anthony whispers.

"Maybe I want you to." Shanette says with a smile while she stroked up and down.

Pulling back, he got down on his knees with Shanette. With a yank, he threw open her blouse. The act was so forceful, her bra busted too. Two large round breasts bounced out. Anthony dove right into sucking her right nipple as he held the left. Laying back, she opened her legs. Pulling down his pants, he placed himself in between her thighs.

Feeling the tip of his bare penis against her twat, she says softly "we need a condom Anthony."

"And I need to feel this pussy cum on my dick." Pushing himself deep inside her and kissing her lips he began fucking her. Slow and steady was their rhythm. All positions were tried there on the floor in the hallway. But while he pounded that pussy and sucked her toes, he felt a massive amount of cum rushing up to be unleashed. "Shanette! I'm coming and I do not want to pull out."

"I don't want you to, but you have to baby. Put it in my mouth. Cum in my mouth." Shanette said passionately.

With one more hard deep thrust Anthony growled, then he pulled the monstrous piece of meat out and sprayed her stomach with his cum. "I didn't baby. Your belly got the full load."

"Yes, but I wanted to taste you like you did me." She said with pouting lips.

Then without hesitation he leaned to her stomach and licked up some of his own cum. Moving over top of her he kissed her. Excepting the extra fluid in his mouth they continued to kiss passionately. "

"Ummm. Yummy." She said as she swallowed.

“Shanette. Shanette. Bitch, you hear me?”

Blinking wildly, she said “What? What you call me?"

She heard again, “Bitch. Wake up. You fell asleep on me?”

Now realizing what’s happening. Shanette becomes aware that she fell asleep on the phone while talking to Dominece about the date. And during her sleep, she had a very, very wet dream. Clothes half on, she drifted off changing clothes. "Dom, I have to call you in the morn. I'm all messed up."

"Ok Bitch. Don't soak your bed toying that cat!" Dominece said laughing as she hung up.

Saying out loud after putting down her phone, "Too late about soaking the bed, and no toy was needed. Damn! If he fucks like that in dreams, I can't imagine what he would do for real!"

Chapter X

Troubled Emotions

It was the start of another work week, and Shanette was on the way to the agency. Only this morning she was floating on a cloud with a heavy heart. Delightful about how the date went with Mr. Regal and worried about Mrs. Donovan's mystery condition. How will she tell her that she heard that private conversation and how will she react? Will she confide in her and include her? Or will Ms. Donovan fire her? As Shanette continued to tussle with the different scenarios, she noticed Victor the security guard get up and move quickly towards her.

"No no, no. Not today Victor. I have a lot on my...,"

Cutting her off, he says "Someone in your office was just rushed out in an ambulance!"

Eyes wide and mouth open, she barely stuttered out "What, Who, When?"

"About 15 minutes ago. It may have been your boss. Don't worry, I locked up the office. Get your ass to Grape Hill Hospital, and call or text me what's going down."

Shanette turned, ran back out of the door and back to the garage to her car. On the way to the hospital, she called Dominece knowing well that she couldn't answer. But she would see she had a voice mail. Then she tried calling Toni Voss.....no answer. Jack Arms' phone just kept ringing. She kept trying them both till she pulled up at Grape Hill.

Entering, she saw a familiar face Robin Lock. Rolling her eyes and saying “Damnit,” Shanette had forgotten that her friend Robin was head nurse there. Dashing to the head nurses station, she asks Robin “Was my boss brought in today?"

"You mean, Donovan? Vikki Donovan?" Robin asks, seeing and hearing her friends panic. "Yes! She was brought in by ambulance a half hour ago. Signed in by a white man with an accent, and a heavy set short black woman. Both of them seemed extremely worried."

"They were Toni Voss and Jack Arms. They work in the office with me. Where are they? How is she?"

"You know I'm not supposed to give out info to non-family members, but for you I'll see what I can find out. Your coworkers are in waiting room C on the 5th floor Intensive care unit." Robin tells her friend in a whispering voice.

As Shanette came through the waiting room door, Jack and Toni stood up. The two women rushed at each other and hugged tightly. Jack came towards them, and Shanette said "I heard part of the conversation you three were having. How is she? What is wrong with her?"

Jack embraced them both declaring they are really not sure. Could be numerous possibilities. "Shanette dear, worst case scenario is....cancer. Vikki is a tough old bird though. Prayers, medicine and old fashion care, and she will be just fine."

The sincerity in Jacks voice seemed to calm the women, but it was for just that. Looking up and away he had a tear run down his cheek. Just then Mrs. Donovan's doctor came in. "Are the Donovan family members in here?"

"Her husband died long ago and she had no kids, but we are her work family. That's about as close as you're going to get doc!" Toni told him.

"Well in that case, Mrs. Donovan is being moved to a private room as we speak. You'll be able to go in and see her in about an hour." The doctor said using a very even toned bed side voice.

Drying her eyes, Shanette asks "What is it? I mean what happened to her? Everyone is grown here. Is it cancer?"

"And you are ma'am?"

"I'm Shanette Tolls, and Vikki Donovan has been and is like an adopted mom to me."

Allowing a grin to appear on his face, he announces "We are not sure Ms. Tolls. She has lost a large amount of blood. We are running various tests. But we can almost assuredly rule out cancer. We believe it may be a heart issue. Though not as menacing as cancer, it is a very serious matter."

"Thank you so much doctor. Just knowing cancer is not a probable answer is a huge relief" Jack says.

Then a tall figure appears in the window looking through. Then he walks through the door. Anthony Regal. "Shanette, I came as soon as the guard down stairs told me about Vikki."

Jack Arms stepped in front of Shanette, "Mr. Regal! This is a very inappropriate time to talk business. Whatever dealings that were in progress will have to be postponed."

"Mr. Arms. This is not a business stop. Ms Tolls and I have been in contact with each other on a personal level. And the business deal I have with The Donovan Agency is in full forward progress. So now, Mrs. Donovan and I are friends and I am here to see about my friend."

Unfolding his arms, he extended his hand to Regal. "Any friend of Vikki's is a friend of mine and Toni's. Thank you for coming."

Anthony moves to Toni and hugs her and announces, “If there is anything I can do for you or the company, consider it done." They all sit down and await news on Vikki's condition together.

Chapter XI

What Now?

It's been close to a month now since Vikki Donovan was rushed to the hospital. Her condition has improved, but she's not free and clear yet. Any stress could cause a relapse or worse. By her doctors and coworkers orders, she was put on immediate bed rest. The business continued on, but no new clients and no new models were approved. Clients are Vikki's responsibility and the models Jack's. Out of respect for her, he wouldn't do his job till she could do hers.

It's Friday, and Shanette really needed to unwind. Not wanting to abuse Regal's generosity with the free entry and V.I.P room, the spot tonight would be club Frost. Club Frost wasn't one of the top clubs, but it had great music and cheap bottom shelf drinks. Robin couldn't make it out, because she was called in to work a double shift at the hospital. Dominece came, but had to leave early due to overtime work the next morning. Dom loved to club, but loved extra money more. So that left Shanette and Anita. The two women weren't close like sisters. They were more like 1st cousins. They got along great. Usual girl arguments that was always smoothed over before anyone went home. Only thing is, Shanette knew to never bring a well to do guy around her. Because as soon as she went to the restroom, Anita is the kind of woman who would "accidentally" expose a titty or give a pussy flash to the man. Shanette was a very pretty woman, but naked lady parts trumps a beautiful clothed woman 8 out of 10 times to a single man.

After dancing for at least an hour straight, Shanette went to find an empty booth while Anita got some drinks. More than likely free drinks due to the outfit Anita was wearing. After a few moments of winks and arm brushes two drinks were slide next to Anita. As she turned to say Thank You, her eyes flew wide open and her jaw dropped. Without actually speaking, she says......Pit!!

"What up girl? How you been? That ass sure looking tasty. What a brother got to do to get back in that?" Pit says trying to stand like a pimp.

Looking around for security just in case, Anita slow moves away from the bar and answers "Hello Chris. I told you previously that we couldn't go out again. You're just too much man for me." Knowing he has erratic mood swings she chooses her words carefully. Making sure not to set him off, she made sure to compliment him and reject him nicely. She had evaded him for the past couple of months. But here he is, right in her face, with alcohol in his system....shit!!!

"I'm too much man for any woman. I understand why you could be intimidated by me. My money is straight again, and I want you again." Chris says.

Anita backs away a little faster now. "It was good seeing you again. I really have to go now. Take care of yourself." She then turns and goes back to the table with Shanette.

Anita flops down flustered and sweating. Motioning to the waiter, she asks for a triple cognac no ice. Shanette asks what happened, and if she was ok. She says, "I don't know yet. Pit is here and walked up on me." Shanette grabbed her purse and started to stand, but Anita reached out and stopped her, "Sit down honey. I think it's ok. He didn't act an ass."

"Damn dude, who was that? Baby girl is fine!"

Pit turned to the guy standing next to him at the bar. "Ahh that's Anita. I use to beat that pussy up awhile back man. Good shit, but the head was sorry. See that waiter right there?"

"Yeah."

"He's taking a drink back to Anita's friend over there at the table. I peeped them about an hour ago."

"How you know it wasn't for her?" The buddy asked.

"She likes those fruity drinks. Watch my game and take notes playa. I'm going to buy her a drink that she likes, put this little pill in it and wear that ass out tonight. "

"Dude! Ain't that considered rape or at least a form of it?" The guy asks shocked by what he just heard.

"Shit after this. It won't matter. All it does is turn up that pussy heat till they damn near rape a man. Hell, her partner looks good to. Get your game tight, you might be in some ass yourself." Pit said sounding very cocky. And with that, he buys the drink, drops the pill in without anyone seeing, slips the waiter a $10 bill and turns back to his bud to continue their previous conversation.

Anita finally calms down, after telling Shanette about Pit and realizing that he isn't coming over and starting a butt load of shit. Just then the waiter came over with a tall colorful drink. The two girls look at each other and the drink then each other again. "When you order that?" Anita asks.

"I thought you did." Shanette answers.

"Must be from that damn Pit. Son of a bitch knows his drinks. But I'm off cognac now, you want it?" Anita says as she eases the drink towards Shanette.

"Well then......bottoms up bitch. Here to Chris's crazy ass and generosity."

The 2 woman Crew go back to partying and dancing. After about a 1/2 hour, Shanette began to act real strange. Dancing on guys like a paid stripper, sweating heavily and talking like a porn star. Shanette could cut loose and let her hair down with the best of them, but this behavior is very unNette like.

Chris.....Pit had been talking to Anita for a couple minutes now while Shanette had been dancing. He asked how the drink was and if she was feeling warm yet. She said no and that she had given the drink to Shanette. Exhaling deeply he turned to look at Anita's friend on the dance floor. There she was grinding on some dude. That's when he noticed it was his buddy Devin getting the benefits of the drink. Chris smiled and said to himself "at least D will get some guaranteed ass."

On the floor, Shanette pooped her ass on Devin, rubbed her pussy on his leg and flashed her breast a time or two. Devin knew she must have drunk the drink when they slow danced and she unzipped his pants and stroked his penis. He asked if she had a man and she said yes, but he's out of town. She said she felt strange and that for some reason she was extra horny. He offered to accompany her outside to get some air. She said that sounds like a good idea.

Outside, Devin lead Shanette to his car. In the backseat of his car, there he kissed her and caressed her breast. That sent her over the top. He pulled his dick out and she sucked it like a kid on a Popsicle. Her vision was blurry and speech horrific. In Shanette's mind, she was in a car with Anthony. She even called Devin, Anthony. To him being called another man's name didn't matter right now, ass was available. He put on a condom and fucked Shanette like a prostitute. He even fucked her in the ass. She was so drunk and out of it that she was numb. They were so loud passers stopped to watch.

Just as Devin came, the crowd cheered and Anita moved through the crowd looking for her friend. Stumbling out of the car, Shanette was greeted by Anita and she said "You dirty whore, must have been some good dick for all this."

Through all the sweating during sex, some of the effects of the pill had worn off. She said "What? I just had sex with my man."

"No bitch! You had sex with a man, but not your man."

The words shocked Shanette a little closer to reality. Focusing on the man she just had sex with, she said "Oh Fuck No! No No No No! What have I done? Anita what am I going to tell Anthony? Take me home! Please! Now PLEASE! And she busted in tears. Even once she got home, she continued to cry.

At about 4am she got a text from Anthony. It said thinking about you. Hope you have been doing the same. She took the phone and threw it in the hall and fell of the bed in uncontrollable tears.

Chapter XII

Loose Lips

This is not the direction her life should be going in Shanette thought. Great job in jeopardy because the owner is sick and confined to her bed. The man of her dreams has to remain in contact with his ex-girlfriend because she manages one of his clubs. Not to mention she is a sexual ex. There is a difference between an ex you just dated and an ex that you had sex with. Now to put the stink on the shit cake, she had sex with some asshole in the back seat in front of a crowd no less. All because she drank a loaded drink meant for someone else. Possibly Anita, but Pitt never went that low to get her. Fuck!!!!! How is she 'gonna tell Anthony about the car mistake. Should she even tell him? She knew her guilt would be too much to bare not to tell him. They had only been dating now for a couple months, but those few months has been better than any relationship she ever had. Too soon to say I love you, but she was at a point where she would make a run for him in her pajamas.

The Crew came to Shanette's cause this was a true crisis that needed to be addressed. After she told all the girls about what happened in the club and afterwards, all had a different opinion about what she should do. Dominece being the heat of a flame said, they should find the dude and bust that ass. Robin being a level headed mother hen said report it as a rape. Even though she was drugged, she figured she went willingly and undressed herself. Plus she didn't want to suffer the embarrassment of questioning by the police. Anita was there and saw the pain, disappointment and shame on her face. Yet, she said if the dick was good just throw the encounter in the closet and file it under shit happens.

"Bitch!! Are you fucking nuts or just a natural hooker? She was drugged and taken advantage of. What if it happened to you trick? Dominece yelled at Anita,

"If it was me, I would have got something out of it. Some money, jewelry or at least a note paid." Anita replied with bold arrogance.

"Heffa, have you lost your motherfuckin mind? She's not a hoe like you. Your dignity may have a price, but that doesn't mean hers does!" Said Robin coming from the kitchen with a fresh bottle of wine.

The other girls turned and looked at her eyes wide and mouth gaped. Dominece got up and slapped a high five to her. Shanette smiled and told her she hadn't heard her curse since college. Anita smiled and said, "Damn girl. Where has that been stewing at?"

Robin apologized to Anita for swearing at her, but assured her the rest of the statement was meant. Anita said, "No problem. I speak my mind. So how can I be mad at you for speaking yours? Even if it was with a potty mouth." Robin laughed and placed the bottle and glasses on the coffee table.

After a couple bottles and a few select movies, the Crew was in a lack of a better word or phrase, twisted. They all talked about their private issues that's been bugging them. Shanette's issues were already on the table and discussed during the first two bottles. Dominece declared that she had been seeing a man for the last couple months and that he may or may not be married. Robin said Gerald has been real secretive lately and has been hanging out with Frank more than her. And she is wondering if he may be sugar filled or curious. Anita's only issue was that her new guy may be passing on a promotion at his job. He rather stay where he is at because he loves what he's doing. And the new job will mean unwanted and unneeded stress. Who cares about his stress? It's more money. Selfish to the core.

The more they compared problems, the more they drank. The more they drank, the more they aired what was on their mind. In between all the wine and talk, Shanette completely forgot that Anthony was due back tonight. And he was coming to see her before going to his hotel, where he rented a room for weeks at a time.

Driving in his rental on the way to see Shanette, he smiled as he thought about the news he was going to tell her. He had decided to move to her city so they could be a couple full time. Not over the phone or when he came back to handle business. This was a big step for him. He hadn't considered being serious with a women since he and Michelle, his ex and club manager broke up. Sexually she was hard to resist, but he was and always had been an emotional man. If the heart says no the body has to follow, and now his heart is saying Shanette. This woman makes him smile just by thinking about her. In her presence, he feels so comfortable and not afraid to be himself. Be a little silly, which is in his true nature. He also listens to her. Being able to change her emotions. Knowing what to say, if she is feeling over whelmed or lift her spirts if her day was not so good. Anthony was not in love, but was willing to commit to Shanette and let love come. He pulled into a space in the parking lot and called Shanette. He never just showed up. He had respect for her privacy and only came if he was invited. Sometimes a woman needs alone time.

Inside, Shanette's phone buzzed. Anita had it talking to Frank while she had another guy on hold on her phone. She clicked over and said come on in. When he entered all the girls were laughing and falling over. He asked, “What did I walk in on?” Robin sat up and said, “That Fool Anita forgot which guy was on hold on which phone. Talked terribly about Frank to Frank.....hilarious!”

Shanette said, "Come sit down here baby. Want some wine? Oops! No more wine. Want a beer?"

"No thanks. I'll just steal a bottled water, but before that I think I'll steal a kiss. "

Dominece and Robin said that's too cute. Anita rolled her eyes still feeling the sting of embarrassment. Looking at Anita, Shanette told her don't be mad, choose one guy and stick with him. No man will respect her if she opens her legs when he opens his wallet. That got a huge laugh from the other girls and a that's true from Anthony in the kitchen. That didn't mix well with her being embarrassed and full of wine.

"Well at least I fuck for profit. You fucked a dude for a drink. Guess you are ignoring the other night since your boo is here now," Anita blurted out wanting Shanette to feel worse than her.

Shanette looked at her and dropped her glass then looked at Anthony in the kitchen doorway. He choked, and said "What? Would you repeat that?" as he came and sat down next to Shanette.

"Miss Advice here got drunk in a club the other night and started dry humping some guy on the dance floor. After that she went missing for a while. I went outside and saw her getting fucked backseat style in the parking lot. Oh and so did about 30 other people. It was quite a show. She said someone pilled her drink, but we had the same waiter all night."

Staring at Shanette with watery eyes now, he asked if this was true. She began to cry and fell on the floor next to him. Robin teared up too, and Dominece let off a cursing tirade towards Anita. Anthony stood up and pulled Shanette up. "I guess it is true then." A cold streak went from his neck to his knees. He almost buckled, but he didn't want Shanette and the girls to see how hurt he was.

"You better not hit her bitch ass!" Anita felt she needed to say.

Before he could respond, Robin said, "He ain't like the fools you deal with. You inappropriate fucking whore!"

"I have never and will never strike a female. Now ladies, I believe I need to be going. Good night ladies."

As he went out the door, very quickly. Shanette ran after him. Saying I'm so sorry please let me explain don't go yet. He turned and stopped.

"Why didn't you tell me after it happened? Why did I have to find out this way? Thought I meant more to you. Thought we meant more to each other, or am I the only one who feels this way? I came to tell you that I was moving here for good. Moving here for you. Moving here to let our hearts grow together. I wanted us! I feel bad for you, because you said you were drugged. But if you didn't feel right, you should have left."

"I know. My mind was saying it was you, but my body...."

"Your body was enjoying him. Good bye Shanette. I'll call the office to check on Mrs. Donovan."

"What about me Anthony?" Shanette asks not bothering to wipe her tears away.

Taking a deep breath and knowing this might add more pain to her, but he needed to say it. "What about you?" He got in his car and raced off.

Going back in, Robin and Dominece hugged her and said, "Do you need anything? Can we do anything for you?" She said, "No, I just want to be alone."

Anita said, "I didn't mean to say all that and salt your game or drag that skeleton out of the closet...."

Before she finished her sentence, Shanette looked at her with red teary eyes and growled. "Get the fuck out of my house. You dick sucking whore, before I beat the living shit out of you, Bitch!"

Chapter XIII

Bad to Worse

It has been 7 months since the disaster that occurred at Shanette's place between her, Anthony and Anita. After she sobered up, Anita apologized to Shanette many times over. She accepted it after about the 30th time, but she promised herself that from now on information with Anita will be limited. Anthony on the other hand accepted Shanette's apology, but did it cold. Gave one word responses. Didn't call her and often ignored her calls. She wanted to fix her relationship with him, but he told her there was nothing to fix any more. He had let her into his heart, and she burnt it to the ground. The sex with another man hurt. It was the not telling him that she went through such a horrific event. He felt he could have done something, anything for her. Help find out what she was given, who the guy was with Pit, or just held her to let her know she has a man in her life that would be there when she needed him. Shanette stole this opportunity from him. The act showed him that she didn't trust him with truths, and that she had no problems keeping secrets from him. He may have been wrong to feel this way, but that's how he felt.

Anthony stayed out of town mostly now. The last time she saw him was when he came into the agency to tell Jack and Toni that he would be sending a rep for him from now on. That day he passed her in the hallway and the only thing he said was, “Excuse me Ms. Tolls” as he moved past her. This hurt more than a slap to the face. Seeing tears well up in Shanette's eyes, Toni and Jack came over to console her and keep her from breaking down crying.

Another Monday back to work without Mrs. Donovan and without a call or appearance of Anthony Regal. Jack Arms had done a wonderful job keeping the agency steady while Vikki was out sick. Her condition had improved slightly, but slight improvement is better than none. Shanette had talked to her briefly on the phone. Her voice was weak, but she tried to put up a good front. Toni Voss helped Jack every step of the way. Vikki was like a sister to her so Vikki's absence was extremely hard on her. Jack being a man. British man. He absolutely could not show how emotionally draining Mrs. Donovan’s sickness was on him. Even Victor the security guard had stopped being such an ass. Actually being concerned about everyone. Then he would be his old self once a big ass or big chest strolled pass his view.

Shanette tried to woo new clients, but her mind was so distracted she couldn't nail all of them. With the Crew in a mini crisis with her and Anthony, Robin and Gerald possibly being down low, Dominece fucking a younger possibly married man and Anita being nothing but a bitch, Shanette needed some cheering up. All clubs were out of the question now because of Pit, his friend and that damn drugged drink. So....against her better judgment, she agreed to a meeting slash date with Victor. He asked if she could come by for a late, late drink and possibly go to a new midnight snack joint called Sugar Shack. It didn't open till 10pm and closed at 6am. For those people who craved sugar late at night. Cakes, ice cream and varieties of sweet coffees. The idea seemed ok. What could it hurt? Of course he offered his sex services as an alternative, then said, 'I'm just joking.' She knew he was serious, but no way was he going to get any of her ass. To be on the safe side she called Dominece to let her know when she was leaving and she would call as soon as she got home.

Shanette got dressed, grabbed her keys and said aloud, "Am I really this desperate now? What the fuck am I doing?" And walked out the door.

Chapter XIV

Making Things Clear

It had been a long day with no clients. Anthony was in town and he still wanted nothing to do with her. Victor the security guard didn't even harass her. Guess he was either embarrassed or mad from last night. Her guess was embarrassed. Only bright spot so far was Dominece called and invited her to lunch. A lunch date with your bestie can always make things better. She told Jack and Toni she was going out for lunch downtown with Dom. They both told her take your time, it's a slow day.

By the time Shanette got to the restaurant, Dominece was waiting at a table with a glass of something in front of her. Talking to herself, she said "Oh Lord, I truly hope that isn't a drink, and why isn't she at work?" When Dom saw her friend, she rose out of her seat and hugged her. As they both sat, Shanette looked over at Dominece's glass. And before she could ask, she told her it was just a regular mango ice tea. Relieved, she smiled and sat back finally putting her purse down next to her in the booth.

Picking up a menu, Shanette says, "I appreciate the lunch invite, but why aren't you at work?"

"Bitch, I fucked up big this time!"

"What? What happened? What you do?" Shanette asked dropping the menu.

"My young tasty at work. Well I saw him get in a car this morning with some bitch. So I went over and called his ass out. His chick got out and said, "What was my problem?" He gets out and says, 'It ain't what it looks like or what I think.' So I popped the shit out of him. She rushes me and we tussle in the parking lot."

"So he was married and you caught him?"

"Not exactly. Turns out he's not married. The chick is his little sister and she has been staying with him till her apartment is ready. She came by to drop his key off 'cause she would be working late."

"Damn girl, that's good news and fucked on your part at the same time."

"What's worse is, we got suspended for a week at work for fighting on company property. But he ain't mad at me. He likes that I'm a let's get down with it chick."

Laughing, Shanette says "You and your luck bitch. Get your man, but no pay for a week."

Giggling herself, Dominece replied "Ain't that the damn truth!"

As they ate, they continued to discuss many things. Eventually Regal came up and what would Shanette do if she ran into him. Dom told her that big brother Gerald told her that Anthony would be in town from Friday to Monday to officially thank the Donovan Agency for such a great partnership. The contract for the models to be in the club had ended. Business was as good here as it was in any other city. The Agency management would still receive free entry and models used would get a special I.D. for discounted entry.

Shanette looked at her and declared, “Today is Monday! Shit! He may already be gone by now. If not, he could be anywhere in the city. With him not answering my calls, finding him would be impossible.

"I really need to talk to him. If we are really over, I don't want him hating me." Shanette says with a pale look on her face.

Dominece takes a sip from her glass and almost chokes. "My luck must be rubbing off on you."

"Why you say that?" Shanette asks after cleaning her mouth with a napkin.

With a smile, Dominece leans back and points outside "Mr. impossible to find is across the street waiting on a cab."

Snapping her head around, Shanette looks outside. Without a word of goodbye, she darts out the restaurant. As soon as she reached the street, she could see him get in the back seat. Yelling his name......loudly "Anthony! Anthony please wait." Suddenly, she trips and falls on the curb. A motor revs up and the sound of a car taking off. She sat there and cried. Sadly, no one even helped her up or even asked her if she was alright. Then she felt the presence of someone behind her.

Through teary eyes, she saw a figure kneel down to her. Raising her arm to pull herself up on their shoulder she says, "Dominece. He's gone. And I never got to say I'm sorry in person."

Then the figure said, "it's ok girl, we'll road trip to all of his clubs if we have to, to find him."

The woman stands up and bumps into a guy. "I always did hate to see a beautiful woman cry." Wiping the tears from her eyes, the man's image becomes clear. It was Anthony Regal. "Are you alright? We pulled off, and I saw a woman fall. After seeing it was you, I gave the cab to someone else."

"Please let me talk to you Anthony."

"How could I say no to such a pretty lady in tears?!" Regal said touching her face.

Chapter XV

It's Me or No One

Shanette sat in the living room of her town house waiting on Anthony to arrive. After the brief talk they had on the curb downtown, he agreed to sit down with her and listen to what she had to say. So, she went back to work and he went back to his hotel room. Now here, she sat hoping and praying that Anthony would indeed come by. She picks the phone up, looks at it, then sits it back down. She did this several times until there was finally a knock at the door. Blushing and heart pounding, she answered the door. Anthony stood in the entrance and asked, "May I enter?" His face was emotionless. At least there was no anger in his voice or eyes she thought.

As they sat, she looked into his eyes and tried to speak, but the only thing she could do was tear up. He reached and held her hand. Shanette raised his hand to her face. Feeling the touch of his skin against hers comforted her.

"I am so sorry! I never ever meant to hurt you. I..I.." Shanette said with true pain in her voice.

"I know that Shanette. All I wanted was to be there for you, but you never gave me the chance."

"I......""I......"

"Let me finish. It was horrible what happened to you and it wasn't your fault. None of it. I am man enough to know your heart wasn't in that. Hell! Your mind wasn't even in it. I just wanted and needed you to trust me. But that was then and this is now."

"I should have done that. Can you forgive me? Can we start again?" She said softly laying her head on his shoulder.

Anthony raised up from the couch and moved to the door. Turning back towards her he says “Us? Try again? I don't think so.”

Shanette dropped her head, stood up and said, "I understand.”

"How can we start again if we never really ended? We needed time to get to this point. Now everything is on the table out in the open."

Shanette ran to him and hugged him and then kissed him.

"I love you Shanette Tolls. Wow, I have never said that to anyone outside my family. Tell you what. Let me go to the club and make sure all is well, then I will pick up some dinner and we will discuss our future."

"Sounds perfect, and I love you too Anthony," Shanette stood and watched him leave in his club manager’s car.

Later that evening at Regal's club , he had just finished his meeting which made the manager very happy. Mr. Regal would still be able to make frequent appearances. Regal stood looking out at the packed house through a huge one way mirror that only appeared as a wall on the other side. In the crowd, he noticed a couple arguing by the side bar.

"Why you tripping girl? Quit all this bullshit. You know damn well it should still be you and me. My money ain't strained no more," the guy said.

"Fuck you, your little bank account and your little dick. First of all you ain't that cute, your clothes are old, you punk ass truck is over 2 years old and it's not even the top of the line. You're crazy as fuck, you hound a bitch. Why you think we call you Pit?!"

To end this she moves closer and says in his ear, "every time after we fucked, I went to the bathroom and fucked myself with a 5 inch dildo. That's two more inches more than you."

Backing away she said, "Right now, all you can do for me is give me this little tired ass drink you keep pushing in my face."

"You drunk ass bitch! Trust me! You'll be sucking me by nights end," Pit says with a devilish smirk on his face.

The two were beginning to cause the other club goers to become uncomfortable. Security had started to slowly move in when Regal came and put his hand on a guard's shoulder and patted his own chest to say, he got it. "Excuse me Anita, are you alright? Let me take you home. Seems like you've had a little too much tonight."

As Regal and Anita turned to leave the club, Pit grabbed her arm and asked, "Who the hell is this dude?"

She turned and mouthed, "He's the owner of the club and my new man." She then snatched away from him and took Regal's arm and walked away.

"Whatever bitch, you mine."

Anthony Regal once again borrowed his manager's car to take Anita home. He could have called a cab for her, but she was too drunk and would feel terrible if something happened to her like what happened to Shanette. Especially if he could have done something to avoid it. So as they drove along she slurred out directions to her place. While she talked she rubbed on his chest and his leg. She even exposed her chest to him. Being the gentleman he was, he keep his eyes on the road. It was hard. Damn hard, and so was trying not to look at her. He noticed a car tailgating him when she leaned against the door and pulled up her skirt. No panties. She placed her finger in her pussy and asked if he wanted a taste. Out the window, he saw the name of her apartments. Thank

God. He pulled to the lot and parked by a lone tree. Getting out and going around to the passenger side, he opened the door, then he saw headlights speeding directly towards them.

Chapter XVI

Explanations

Robin began her night with the hopes of it being slow, but expecting the worst. She checked in with the other nurses and made her rounds checking clip boards and looking in on patients. Just making sure everyone was comfortable. After a couple hours, a gunshot victim, a child bitten by a dog, 4 broken legs, and domestic violence victim. A small man beaten by his very large wife for buying her an exercise bike. Very uncalled for. Finally sitting down, she texted Gerald. He answered saying he was with Frank and they had something big developing. Then he asked when she was taking lunch, he had something to tell her. With her mind now conjuring up thoughts of her husband coming out of the closet to her. Robin banged the phone on the table a couple times then texted… come now.

Shanette sat on the couch with remote in hand flipping channels. Glancing at the phone to see no missed calls, no texts, and no nothing. Now she looks at the clock on the wall. Where could he be? He left on good terms, so he's not still upset. Taking a deep breath Shanette decided to call the club.

After a brief conversation she found out he left long ago in his car again. The manager really needed his car back too. The guy said Anthony had to rescue her drunk friend from some man at the bar and Mr. Regal was making sure she made it home safe. She knew it wasn't Robin 'cause she wouldn't do that and was at work. Then she called Dominece. She answered cussing....as usual. She wasn't the one. She had been at home having oral sex preformed on her. Information she didn't want, but got anyway. Shanette said a loud "it must be that trick ass bitch Anita. That bitch is after my man!"

After the I'm gonna beat that bitches ass war speech, Shanette got dressed and got in her car calling Anita. No answer. Then she prayed. Please don't let me find out they are fucking. Her ass is beat guaranteed, but his ass may have to be too.

Robin sat in the employee break room letting her mind wonder and Imagine lots of different ways her conversation with Gerald will go. Before her thoughts got too deep, she was brought back to reality by a taping on the Window. Gerard smiled and came in, kissed her on the lips than sat next to her.

"What's wrong babe? Been a rough night already?"

"No actually concerned. Concerned about what you are about to tell me." Robin said with a frown.

Gerald now looking puzzled asked, "Why? What do you think I'm going to tell you?"

"That you're leaving me or worse. You're leaving me for Frank you down low piece of shit!"

He leaned forward and dropped his head. Robin's eyes began to water feeling she was right, but while his head was down Gerald busted out laughing.

"That has to be the funniest thing I've heard all year. Let me clear this all up. I'm not gay! Frank is not gay! Actually Frank is a millionaire investor and we have been in talks about starting a quick engine repair franchise. It was Anthony Regal's idea. He even wanted to invest himself. See baby, I was just trying to make our life better."

"Oh my god Gerald! I am so sorry. Frank is a millionaire? He doesn't look like one."

"Yes. He has backed hundreds of businesses and they all are profitable. By the way, how could you doubt me?" He replied.

"You were always gone with him and started coming home real late. I...I...don't know where my head was at. Can you forgive me?"

With a smile he says, "Repeat my wedding vows to you."

Drying her eyes, she says in a low sexual voice "From the first moment our eyes meet, you had all my attention. The first time you spoke, I was yours. I'm a man who believes in keeping promises. So, I can't promise you the world and everything in it. But I will promise you that the rest of my life I will be trying. No man has ever or will ever love you the way I do."

Gerald said "I'm trying baby." Then he leaned over and kissed his wife.

Then a call came over the intercom. All available nurses to the emergency room. We have a 3 person accident. 1 definite fatality, possible 2. All available nurses to E.R.

"Shit! Back to work I go. Stick around for a while honey, I'll be back."

Robin walked through the hall and glanced at her phone. Shanette had called several times and texted several times. As she entered E.R she looked at the accident victims. All laid motionless. Her eyes widened, and she redialed Shanette.

"Hello Robin. I think that bitch Anita is trying to fuck Anthony...."

Robin cut her off saying, "Anita just came in here in an ambulance. With Pit and Anthony injured too, girl they said 1 is already dead and possibly another. Get here now!!!!"

Dropping the phone, she screamed and tears flowed like a water fall. She hit the gas and raced toward the hospital. "Lord, please let them be alright." She continued to pray the full way there.

After Robin called Shanette, she had a nurse's assistant go get her husband and meet her in the hallway. As she told him who just came in and the condition they were in, Gerald held her. By this time, Shanette arrived calling for Robin.

Not being able to see her man and her friend, Shanette sat in the waiting room with Gerald. Dominece also rushed down. Anita wasn't Dom's favorite person, but she was still a friend. Also she wanted to be there for Shanette.

Soon the police showed up to ask routine questions. They explained to the group that the initial officer report says a witness saw a car driven by Chris Bills (Pit). Mr. Bills apparently aimed his vehicle at the two others in an attempt to run them over. Mr. Regal pushed Ms. Watts back in the car while he took the full force of the hit. The vehicle then hit a tree ejecting Mr. Bills through the wind shield killing him instantly. They then asked relationship between the three. A short time after the police left and the doctor came in.

The doctor said that Pit was D.O.A, and Anita had a concussion from hitting the back of her head on roof of car after being pushed back.

With tears racing down her face, Shanette asked about Anthony. The doctor said he was very sorry.

They tried to save him. He had internal bleeding, collapsed lungs, 5 broken ribs, shattered pelvis, broken spine and cracked skull from his head hitting the hood of the car. There were just too many injuries and he didn't survive. Shanette started to shake. Then she stood up and tried to take a step and fainted.

Shanette awoke at home in her bed alone. She thought everything she just heard and experienced was all a dream. She got up from her bed and went into the living room, and saw all her friends sitting there with a blank look on all their faces. All except Anthony. They came over and hugged her. Vikki Donovan, Toni and Jack was there. Of course Dominece, Robin and Gerald. Victor the security guard was even there. Anita was still in the hospital. They held Shanette as she cried and cried and cried.

Chapter XVII

Moving On

It has been a week since Regal's death. Literally hundreds showed up for his funeral. Friends, family, associates and business partners. Even admirers of his attended. It was beautiful. Celebrity singers and moving speeches about his character. After he was laid to rest and Shanette was lead back to the limo, Anita came up to her apologizing saying she was drunk and he was just looking after her. Rescuing her from Pit in the club, and he saved her life.

Shanette says "I can't be mad at what he did because that was the type of man he was, but you on the other hand. A hoe will be a hoe, and I forgive you for being a back stabbing opportunist bitch with no regard for feelings or friendship." Then she turns her back to Anita.

Dominece steps up to Anita and says, "She may forgive you and your ways, but I don't!" She then draws back and punches Anita directly in the mouth knocking her out cold. Robin stood next to Dominece and laughed. Shanette sat in the limo and smiled. Dom leaned in the limo and ask Shanette if she will be ok?

Taking a deep breath, she said "No." But in time she would be. As the car drove off, Shanette took out her phone and looked at a picture she had of them together. Then she thought to herself, 'Was the short time she had with Anthony, worth all this pain?' saying softly to herself, 'the pleasure of knowing he loved me and I loved him was worth any amount of pain.'

The End